WINNIPEG

SEP 16 2014

0761114 15

PUBLIC LIBRARY

WITHDRAWN

D0604862

Put Me in a Book!

by
Robert Munsch

illustrated by
Michael Martchenko

NORTH WINDS PRESS
New York Toronto London Auckland Sydney
Mexico City New Delhi Hong Kong Buenos Aires

The illustrations in this book were painted in watercolour
on Crescent illustration board.
The type is set in 22 point Adobe Caslon Pro.

Library and Archives Canada Cataloguing in Publication
Munsch, Robert N., 1945-
Put me in a book! / Robert Munsch ; illustrations by Michael Martchenko.

ISBN 978-1-4431-0079-3

I. Martchenko, Michael II. Title.

PS8576.U575P88 2009a   jC813'.54   C2009-905501-5

Text copyright © 2010 by Bob Munsch Enterprises Ltd.
Illustrations copyright © 2010 by Michael Martchenko.
All rights reserved.
No part of this publication may be reproduced or stored in a retrieval
system, or transmitted in any form or by any means, electronic, mechanical,
recording, or otherwise, without written permission of the publisher, North
Winds Press, an imprint of Scholastic Canada Ltd., 604 King Street West,
Toronto, Ontario M5V 1E1, Canada. In the case of photocopying or other
reprographic copying, a licence must be obtained from Access Copyright
(Canadian Copyright Licensing Agency), 1 Yonge Street, Suite 800,
Toronto, Ontario M5E 1E5 (1-800-893-5777).

6 5 4 3 2 1   Printed in Canada   114   09 10 11 12

For Madame O'Dell's class,
North Bay, Ontario.
— R.M.

On their way back from the lake,
Mrs. O'Dell's class saw a man sitting
on a park bench, holding a big book.

"Hi," said Hailey. "What are you doing?"

"I'm trying to finish this book," said the man. "It's a picture book, but I don't know what kid I am going to use in the story."

"Wow!" said Hailey. "Can you put me in the book?"

"Are you absolutely sure you want to be the kid in this book?" said the writer.

"YES!" said Hailey.

"WONDERFUL!" said the writer, and he picked Hailey up, folded her and flattened her, and stuck her in the book.

"WOW!" said Mrs. O'Dell.
"It is a great honour to be in a book."
Then she took everyone back to school, put the book on her desk, and went to tell the principal the wonderful news.

The book started to flip-flop up and down and say, **"Gwackh!"**

Ethan opened the book and said, "Hailey, are you OK? Do you still want to be in this book?

"HELP!" yelled Hailey. "I am folded and scrunched and trapped and stuck, and I want to get out and go home."

"Don't worry," the class said.
"We will get you out."

Rachel tried to scrape Hailey out of the book with a fingernail.

"AHHHHHHHHHHHH!" yelled Hailey. "That hurts!"

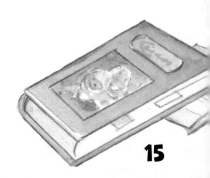

"I know what to do!" said Jakob. "We'll pull the book apart, and Hailey will fall out." So a bunch of kids got on each side of the book, and they tried to pull it apart.

"AHHHHHHHHHHHHH!" yelled Hailey. "You're **STRETCHING** me!"

"Just twist the book and Hailey will pop right out," said Kiku.

They started to twist the book really hard.

"AHHHHHHHHHHHHH!" yelled Hailey. "You're **SCRUNCHING** me!"

"This scraping and pulling and twisting are not working," the kids said. "We have to think of something different."

"Photocopy!" yelled Cole. "We can use the photocopy machine in the staff room and copy Hailey out of the book."

So everyone ran to the staff room and Cole tried to copy Hailey out of the book, but the machine only made pictures of Hailey. The real Hailey was still in the book.

"I know what to do!" said Laura. "We can squeeze her out of the book."

She put the book on the floor and everyone got on top.

For a while nothing happened. Then Hailey's nose sproinged out of the book. The book looked really strange with a nose.

"AHHHHHHHHHHHH!" yelled Hailey. "You're **squishing** me!"

The kids jumped off.

"Well," said Ethan, "at least the principal will be happy."

"And," said Cole, "Mrs. O'Dell LOVES having someone in her class in a book."

"But," said Kiku, "Hailey's mom and dad will not be happy that their kid is stuck in a book! How can you kiss someone goodnight when she is stuck in a book?"

"I've got it!" said Laura. "We can change the ending."

They ran back to the park, took the writer's marker, and wrote at the end of the book:

Then Hailey jumped out of the book and told the writer to find some other kid for his story.

"I don't understand," said the writer. "It is an honour to be in a book."

"RIGHT," said Hailey. She took the marker and wrote:

And then the writer wrote himself into the book. He could not get out and was stuck there FOREVER!

"AHHHHHHHHHHHHHHHH!" yelled the writer from inside the book.

Jakob opened it and said, "Don't worry, it's an honour to be in a book."

Then Hailey gave the book to the librarian.

The librarian LOVED having a writer in the library.

And the book was very popular because it was the only one that bounced up and down on the shelf and yelled,

"HELP! HELP! HELP!"